Superfast Cars™

Viper

Rebecca Hawley

PowerKiDS press™

New York

Published in 2007 by The Rosen Publishing Group, Inc.
29 East 21st Street, New York, NY 10010

First Edition

Editor: Joanne Randolph
Book Design: Ginny Chu
Layout Design: Kate Laczynski
Photo Researcher: Sam Cha

Photo Credits: Cover, pp. 1, 12, 16, 20 © Getty Images; pp. 4, 6, 8, 10 © www.shutterstock.com; pp. 14 © David Taylor/Allsport/Getty Images; p. 18 © Jeff Kowalsky/AFP/Getty Images.

Library of Congress Cataloging-in-Publication Data

Hawley, Rebecca.
   Viper / Rebecca Hawley. — 1st. ed.
      p. cm. — (Superfast cars)
   Includes index.
   ISBN-13: 978-1-4042-3644-8 (library binding)
   ISBN-10: 1-4042-3644-9 (library binding)
   1. Viper automobile—Juvenile literature. I. Title.
   TL215.V544H39 2007
   629.222'1—dc22
                                    2006027224

Manufactured in the United States of America

Contents

Meet the Dodge Viper. Many people use the Viper for street racing and other kinds of racing.

What Is a Fast Car?

Step on the gas of a fast car, and you will soon know what a fast car can do. A fast car springs into action. Fast cars are **designed** to move quickly. They are designed to hug the road. They are also designed to look really cool.

There are lots of cars on the road. There are only a few that can be called superfast cars. The Dodge Viper is one of these cars.

Muscle cars, like the Dodge Viper, got their start in America.

Today's Muscle Car

The Dodge Viper is more than just a superfast car. It is also a muscle car. Muscle cars are midsized cars with large, powerful **engines**.

These cars are designed to move quickly. They are bigger and heavier than the common sports car, though. Muscle cars are high-**performance** cars that cost less than other sports cars. The first muscle car was built in the 1960s. The Dodge Viper is a **modern** take on past muscle cars.

Team Viper worked hard to give the Viper a cool look. They also spent a lot of time testing the car to make sure it would be superfast.

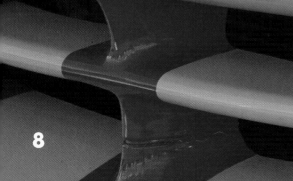

Team Viper

When Dodge decided to make a muscle car, it put together Team Viper. Team Viper was made up of 85 **engineers**. They were picked to come up with a powerful, superfast car.

Team Viper used a large, powerful engine meant for a truck and made it work in a sports car. They also made sure the body of the car would not slow the car down. It did not hurt that they made the car look cool, too.

The first Viper went on sale in 1992. Car lovers were wowed by the power of its engine. This Viper is racing in Germany's 24-hour race.

Start Your Engines!

The Viper made its first appearance as the Indianapolis 500's pace car in 1991. It is a great honor to be picked as the pace car for this well-known race.

A pace car starts the race by setting the **speed** of the first few laps. The car is also sent onto the track if the track is not safe. The pace car makes sure the race car drivers keep their speed down. This makes sure no one gets hurt.

The GTS could go 186 miles per hour (299 km/h). This was 22 miles per hour (35 km/h) faster than the first Viper.

Meet the Viper GTS

In 1996, a faster, better Viper came out. It had more engine power and could brake more quickly. The GTS was also presented in 1996. This Viper had a special roof. The Viper GTS **coupe** had a "double bubble" roof. The bubbles were two small places where the roof was higher. This let the driver and rider wear helmets. The bubbles were added because the superfast car was commonly used for racing.

The Viper GTS-R won a race called the FIA GT Championship against cars of the same kind for many years in a row. It also won its class at the Le Mans 24-hour race many times.

The GTS-R Hits the Track

Makers of superfast road cars often build race cars, too. Dodge is no different. It wanted the Viper to **compete** against other fast cars. Dodge and the French racing team Oreca made the Viper GTS-R.

The GTS-R won a lot of races once it hit the track in 1996. In 1998, it became the first American car in 30 years to win the Le Mans 24-hour race in France. There was no question. The Viper was superfast!

The Viper SRT-10 can reach a top speed of 190 miles per hour (306 km/h). It hits 60 miles per hour (97 km/h) in around 4 seconds.

Street and Racing Technology

Team Viper was put together with some of Chrysler's other engineers and designers. The group became known as Street and Racing **Technology** (SRT). SRT is known for designing the fastest cars for Chrysler, Dodge, Jeep, and Plymouth.

In 2003, SRT gave the Viper a new look and made it run faster and better. They called the new **model** the Viper SRT-10. They have also made an SRT-10 race car that cannot be driven on the road.

The engineers spent many hours in a wind tunnel with the Ram SRT-10. They wanted to be sure that air would not slow the truck down.

A Viper in a Truck

Dodge also made a Viper pickup truck, called the Ram SRT-10. This truck uses the Viper engine, which makes it superpowerful and superfast. In fact, the Ram SRT-10 set the Guinness World Record for world's fastest production pickup truck by going about 154 miles per hour (248 km/h). Trucks are not known for moving at high speeds like this. The Ram SRT-10 came out in 2004.

It is against the law to drive the Tomahawk on the road. The few bikes that have been sold are called rolling art, since they cannot be used.

The Tomahawk

Lovers of the Viper wanted more. The engineers used the Viper engine and the feeling behind Viper to make a motorcycle. The Tomahawk was born in 2003. The motorcycle uses a Viper V10 engine.

The Tomahawk can reach 60 miles per hour (97 km/h) in just over 2 seconds. It is believed that it can reach a top speed of 400 miles per hour (644 km/h)! To handle the power of the Viper engine the motorcycle has four wheels.

What Lies Ahead?

The world of sports cars and muscle cars is a competitive one. Viper will need to keep getting better to stay on top.

No one is sure what is next for the Dodge Viper. The people who love this car are keeping their eyes and ears open, though. They know that whatever Dodge builds next is bound to be cool and superfast. Put on your seatbelts and stay tuned for the next Viper!

Glossary

compete (kum-PEET) To go against another in a game.

coupe (KOOP) A kind of car with two doors and a hard roof.

designed (dih-ZYND) Planned or formed.

engineers (en-juh-NEERZ) Masters at planning and building engines, machines, roads, and bridges.

engines (EN-jinz) Machines inside cars or airplanes that make the cars or airplanes move.

model (MAH-dul) A kind of car.

modern (MAH-dern) Using the most up-to-date ideas or ways of doing things.

performance (per-FOR-mens) The act of carrying out or doing.

speed (SPEED) How quickly something moves.

technology (tek-NAH-luh-jee) The way that people do something using tools and the tools that they use.

Index

C
Chrysler, 17
coupe, 13

E
engineers, 9, 17
engine(s), 7, 9, 19, 21

J
Jeep, 17

L
Le Mans 24-hour race, 15

M
muscle car(s), 7, 9, 22

O
Oreca, 15

R
Ram SRT-10, 19

T
Team Viper, 9, 17
Tomahawk, 21

V
Viper GTS, 13
Viper GTS-R, 15
Viper SRT-10, 17

Web Sites

Due to the changing nature of Internet links, PowerKids Press has developed an online list of Web sites related to the subject of this book. This site is updated regularly. Please use this link to access the list:
www.powerkidslinks.com/sfc/viper/